STAR WARS®
ADVENTURES

The Ghostling Children
NOVEL

STAR WARS®
ADVENTURES

The Ghostling Children

Dave Wolverton

LUCAS BOOKS

SCHOLASTIC INC.

New York • Toronto • London • Auckland • Sydney
Mexico City • New Delhi • Hong Kong • Buenos Aires

ISBN 0-439-45886-2

12 11 10 9 8 7 6 5 4 3 2   3 4 5 6 7 8/0

Printed in the U.S.A.
First Scholastic printing, January 2000

The Ghostling Children

CHAPTER ONE

On the planet Datar, the forest was filled with light. Three moons rode the sky—three disks of the purest silver. They spilled their light like cool water upon the twisted green limbs of the bayah trees. The light dribbled from dark leaves, pooled in the mossy glens, and cascaded in bright droplets on the forest floor.

Creepers dangled from the tree limbs—long vines dripping with huge horn-shaped flowers that opened to the night. On those vines crept blaze bugs, whose backs glowed as bright as coals in a fire. They trundled along the vines from flower to flower, drinking the evening nectar.

The land was nearly silent under the trees. All that could be heard was a mother, gently singing:

> *"Sleep well, my child, tonight.*
> *Though the forest is filled with light,*
> *Close your sweet eyes,*
> *While the sun flies*
> *Over the mountains. Good night."*

Djas Puhr crept through the dark, and stopped to peer toward the source of the singing.

He didn't need his acute night vision on this mission. Datar's moons and the blaze bugs provided ample light. Any bumbling fool could have crept quietly through these woods—except perhaps Djas Puhr's companion, Gondry. Djas Puhr's feet made no sound as he moved. The moss beneath him was as thick as a carpet, and the Ghostlings that lived nearby had cleared all the branches from the forest floor.

Djas Puhr pulled his dark robes close and crept toward the singing. The mother's voice was small and high, like the sound of a stone flute from Djas Puhr's homeworld of Sakiya. He hadn't been prepared for the loveliness of her voice.

The beauty of the Ghostlings was legendary. Their bright skin seemed to glow with a light of its own. Their faces inspired people from many planets, and in the daylight their eyes twinkled like gems.

Ahead, hanging vines were woven into a huge nest, forming a bowl. The nest hung tantalizingly close to the ground, only two meters up. The singing came from inside.

The nest glowed dully in a color that humans cannot see, a color that was given off by the heat of a living body. To Djas Puhr, it looked as though the nest was bathed in faint silvery flames.

All around, farther up in the trees, hung dozens more nests, each the size of a door. Djas Puhr had stumbled upon a Ghostling village.

He thumbed his wrist communicator. "Target acquired. Home in on my beacon. And if you mess this up again, I'll blast you."

From the communicator came an answer—a rumbling growl.

Djas Puhr backed away from the Ghostling village and blended into the trees. He was good at that. The planet Sakiya bred supreme hunters. His black robes and ebony skin allowed him to disappear into the night. His powerful eyes allowed him to see his prey as it slept, even through walls. His keen sense of smell allowed him to hunt creatures that tried to flee.

He did not have to wait long for Gondry to arrive. The giant from the harsh planet Byss came bumbling through the forest, blinking and gaping about with his one huge eye.

Djas Puhr sprung out from under the shadows and grabbed the giant's wrist to keep him from blundering into the village.

"Stop," Djas Puhr whispered. "The target is straight ahead."

The giant squinted his huge eye and moved his head from side to side as he tried to see. "Hwaargh?" *Where?*

"The nest is hanging just off the forest floor, a hundred and fifty meters ahead," Djas Puhr whispered. "There are two Ghostlings inside—a mother and her child. Take only the child. And be careful: The child is worth nothing to our master if you crush it!"

Ghostlings were terribly frail. Merely touching one of the small creatures could bruise it, and a weak blow would shatter its bones. Gondry was such a huge, clumsy creature that Djas Puhr had to constantly remind him to be careful.

Djas Puhr did not like having to repeat his simple instructions. He and Gondry had already gathered six Ghostling children.

Overhead, a creeper hung low. A blaze bug had reached a horn-shaped flower, and now the soft white flower petals caught and reflected the bug's red light so that the whole flower shone like a lamp.

Gondry absently reached up and grabbed the blaze bug, squashing it between two fingers. It burst into flames with a scent like sulfur, burning his fingers like a match. The giant didn't seem to mind the pain.

"Stop that," Djas Puhr whispered. "You'll attract attention. Grab the child, and let's get out of here."

The giant growled, then strode through the thick moss with a *thud*, *thud*, *thud*. Only a cyclops from Byss could have managed to make so much noise.

Fortunately, Gondry didn't wake the Ghostlings— not until he reached into the nest and grabbed the child. A girl suddenly wriggled and cried in Gondry's huge paws. Her mother began to shriek, "Help! Help!"

Gondry pulled the child from the nest.

Ghostling men shouted in horror and appeared at the mouths of their own nests. Though they were small, they moved rapidly. Some of the Ghostlings produced bows and began shooting arrows at

Gondry. Others brought out miniature stun blasters that shot bright blue electric bolts. Still others hurled blaze bugs that shot out a bolt on impact, like fiery little bombs.

Gondry took an arrow in the back and bellowed. The giant yanked a branch of a tree, and the nests began to sway wildly, as if in a storm. The movement ruined the aim of the Ghostlings. The warriors were forced to grab onto their swaying nests to keep from falling.

Gondry plodded off, child in hand, as the rest of the Ghostlings continued hurling their blaze bugs and shooting as best they could.

In moments, the Ghostlings hit Gondry with half a dozen arrows. He took a couple of stun bolts, too.

But cyclopses of Byss were notoriously hard to kill. Gondry could heal himself in moments. He could even regrow arms and legs.

The tiny arrows didn't even slow him. Blaze bugs exploded harmlessly on his skin. He strode rapidly toward the spaceship. Djas Puhr ran to catch him.

They left the Ghostling village far behind.

A few seconds later, they reached the ship of Sebulba the Dug. They rushed up the gangplank. Djas Puhr shouted to his master, "We've got the last child. Let's get out of here!"

Djas Puhr carried the girl down to the hold and placed her in an energy cage with the other Ghostlings they'd caught that night.

She fell down and lay holding her side, as if in pain. Djas Puhr worried that they might have killed her by accident, or perhaps broken some bones. If so, Sebulba would be mad.

Gondry began pulling arrows from his backside.

The ship trembled as the engines started. It lifted off quickly, and tore through the night air. In moments it burst into hyperspace with a familiar *thud*.

Moments later, Sebulba walked into the hold, on his hands.

The Dug inspected the Ghostling. She was a small girl, with hair as silver as moonlight, and piercing violet eyes. Her pointed ears lay back flat against her head. She didn't look very old, perhaps only seven or eight.

When she moved into the light, Djas Puhr could see that she had a huge purple bruise on her arm.

Sebulba began cursing in Huttese. "Gondry, you fool, you could have killed her—and she's the most beautiful of all!" As Sebulba spoke, the feelers over his jaw quivered with anger.

"Hwaree," the giant said, hanging his head. *Sorry.* Gondry's arrow wounds had already closed. He healed that quickly.

"We could throw her back and try again?" Djas Puhr offered. "The Ghostlings are not hard to catch."

"No," Sebulba grumbled. "The bruise will heal, I suspect." The Dug gazed deep into the child's eyes.

"Do you have a name, pretty one?"

To Djas Puhr's surprise, the child spoke to him. "Arawynne," she said. "Princess Arawynne."

"Princess no more—" Sebulba corrected her. "Now, *slave* Arawynne."

CHAPTER TWO

In the city of Mos Espa, the twin suns of Tatooine cut through a darkened doorway of Madame Vansitt's Charm Academy and threw overlapping shadows onto the floor. The day was as hot as an oven outside. A wild man stood in the doorway with sweat beading on his forehead.

A slave girl named Pala knelt on the floor and sneaked a peek at the man before her. He was tall and cruel-looking, with lips turned down in a permanent sneer. His long hair was mostly the color of copper, with streaks of gold and silver thrown in. A knotted leather band held his hair back in a warrior's ponytail.

His strong arms were covered with three-dimensional tattoos of strange beasts, and he wore a long gray tunic made of Firrerean silk, tied at the waist with a golden belt. The belt held a heavy blaster on one side, a long jeweled dagger on the other.

He sneered down at Pala with cruel eyes, and did not say a word as Pala's owner, Madame Vansitt, pointed out Pala's finer selling points. Pala kept her pale green hands folded neatly in her lap, and her golden eyes stared at the floor. She was a Twi'lek from the planet Ryloth, so she tried to make sure that her head-tails didn't twitch nervously.

"Pala is a very cunning child, Lord Tantos," Madame Vansitt said in her best selling voice. "She's been trained in all of the courtly arts—

dance, song, conversation. She'll make a fine wife for your son someday."

"Yes, yes," Lord Tantos said impatiently, scowling down at Pala. "But my son will have no need for *conversation*."

"She is of course adept at espionage," Madame Vansitt pointed out. "She'll make a valuable spy. And she's been trained in the finer arts of bribery and blackmail."

Lord Tantos smiled at Madame unkindly. His eyes were the most amazing color of turquoise. His pale skin was covered with dark blotches, something that was common among Firrereans. "But it is said that you train assassins."

"She's had training in hand-to-hand combat," Madame Vansitt replied. "And she's good with poisons."

"What of *real* battle training? Can she use a blaster, a blade?"

"I don't teach that here. My girls are trained not to attract attention. Such crude weapons are not for women who will be traveling in political circles."

Pala sneaked another look at her prospective buyer. She didn't like this man. He was brutal, dangerous.

Please don't buy me, she thought, hoping the barbarian would pass her by. She knew what he'd want. He'd want her to travel on luxury cruisers or trade ships as a spy. That way, she could tell him which ships were carrying valuable cargo. Then he'd attack the richest ships—while she was on board.

He'd probably have her sabotage the defense and weapons systems before he boarded. But sometimes there would be huge blaster battles. It was dangerous work, far more dangerous than what Pala was trained for.

It was the kind of work that would lead to an early death.

"She's afraid of me," Lord Tantos said, studying Pala. "Terrified."

"Perhaps," Madame Vansitt agreed. "You are, after all, one of the most feared pirate lords in the galaxy. Maybe you should look again at some of the older girls, some who have more courage."

Lord Tantos smiled cruelly. "No, I like it when my slaves are afraid of me. It is a sign of intelligence."

Lord Tantos stepped forward and lifted Pala's chin. He stared for a long moment. Her heart pounded. "I'll pick her up in the morning, the day after tomorrow."

Madame Vansitt clapped her hands as a signal for Pala to go to her room and pack her few belongings. The girl did so quickly, then went to look for her friend, Anakin Skywalker.

CHAPTER THREE

"Anakin!" Kitster shouted as he rushed into the junk shop. "Anakin!"

Anakin was in the back, tearing the power converter out of an old probe droid. He set down his tools and hurried to see his friend.

But before Anakin even got halfway, his owner, Watto, flew up to the door in an angry buzz. He hovered in front of Anakin, cutting off his path, and jabbed an angry finger at Kitster. Watto shouted in Huttese, "I've warned you not to hang around here. Don't bother my slaves while they're working!"

"But, Master Watto," Kitster said, lowering his eyes, "it's important!"

"Hah!" Watto spat. "Kid stuff. Nothing is more important than work!"

"Podracing is," Kitster said. "Sebulba and Gasgano both just flew into the spaceport. They're unloading their racers now. Gasgano has some new engines, and I saw Sebulba's men sneak a big crate into storage. I thought you should know!"

Watto wrinkled his snout, then scratched at the stubble on his chin with grimy fingers. He flapped his wings and looked hard at Anakin. "Baaagh! Find out what's in that crate, and get back here fast. I still have plenty of work for you to do!"

"Wizard!" Anakin shouted. "Thank you, Master Watto." Anakin was happy to get out of the junk shop, at least for a little while.

He pulled on a hooded robe to shield him from the blistering sunlight, then rushed outside with Kitster.

"I don't like that Watto," Kitster confided once they got out the door. "He makes you work too much. Even a slave needs to have some fun."

"I don't mind," Anakin said. It was true. He liked working on things, fixing things. Watto only had Anakin work so much because he was so good at it.

The streets were nearly empty. Most humans and other creatures couldn't bear the midday suns, so they rushed from the shelter of one cool building to another. Only a few eopies clustered in the shadows of the buildings, while Jawas ambled about. Anakin prided himself on the fact that he could bear the heat better than most humans. Maybe that was because he'd been on Tatooine so long.

In practically no time, they reached Mos Espa's docking bay. The white pour-stone buildings gleamed in the sunlight, hurting Anakin's eyes.

Inside the port, the shade felt cool and luxurious. Kitster led Anakin to the docking bays, to Gasgano's Podracer. Anakin scanned it quickly. It had a new engine and a couple of components had been rebuilt. "Aw, there's nothing important here," Anakin said quickly.

"You sure?" Kitster asked.

"Yeah," Anakin replied. It wasn't that he'd inspected the Podracer that closely—he could just *feel* that there wasn't anything new.

The boys rushed over to Sebulba's huge freighter. Sebulba's pit crew milled outside the ship, while droids unloaded small crates.

Sebulba was the star of the Podracing circuit. He always traveled with a crowd of agents, managers, lawyers, bodyguards, and mechanics. He had chefs to feed him and Twi'lek dancing girls to massage him before a race. Slaves carried his baggage.

"Cool!" Anakin said as he gaped at the spectacle. Sebulba's freighter was so big it could have hauled three Podracers.

Spectators crowded around the ship—slaves, curious competitors, and fans. Some burly Gamorrean guards in armor kept the onlookers back.

Anakin and Kitster expertly wiggled through the crowd until they were up front. Anakin's friends were already there—a young girl named Amee, a Rodian named Wald, a Bothan boy with long whiskers named Dorn, and a slender Twi'lek girl named Pala.

Anakin tried to edge up as close as he could to the ship. One green-skinned guard wrinkled his piggy snout and snarled, motioning to keep back. He bared his tusk-like teeth at Anakin and brandished a club.

As repulsorlift jacks raised Sebulba's Podracer from its berth, Anakin gazed up at it from below. In a glance, he could tell that something about Sebulba's Pod had changed. He could *feel* it.

Sebulba waved at the crowd and began to stroll off, while his entourage followed. Before he left, he bared his teeth at Anakin in a menacing smile. "Ready to lose another race, filthy slave?"

"Not to you," Anakin said.

Sebulba laughed and shouted at the pit crew that was lowering the vehicle, "Watch my Podracer carefully. Some young thief might steal something." Sebulba shot Anakin a dirty look, then laughed again and walked away.

Anakin fought back his anger. He'd never stolen anything in his life!

He stared at the Podracer. Pods were fairly simple vehicles. The huge engines were mounted to a chassis just big enough for the driver. All the power went to hurtling the racer over the ground as fast as possible. The machines weren't built with backup systems or safety features.

Anakin studied Sebulba's Pod. It had the same engines as last time, and the same housing. Anakin noticed a peculiar sheen on some chrome. "Wow, look at that!" Anakin suddenly exclaimed. "He's got new stabilizers—Kuat 40-Zs. Those are loads better than anything I've got!"

While Wald nodded at this, Pala didn't seem to react. She seemed to be holding her breath nervously.

Anakin turned toward her. Pala's dark yellow eyes looked as hot as a blaster's flash. Her mouth was drawn down in a tight line, and her twin headtails were lashing back and forth, twitching anxiously. Her pale greenish-blue face seemed flushed.

"What's wrong?" Anakin asked. He took her hand, suddenly worried.

"I've been sold," Pala said. The news shocked Anakin. She'd been his friend for as long as he could remember.

"Sold?" Kitster asked. "How come? Did you do something wrong?" Gardulla the Hutt owned Kitster, and was always threatening to sell him to the glitterstim miners if he didn't shape up. Amee, Wald, and Dorn all huddled close to listen.

Pala shook her head *no*.

"If I know Pala," Dorn said, his long eyebrows raising up to emphasize his point, "she got sold for doing something *right*."

"But—" Kitster objected, "Madame Vansitt can't sell her. She's not old enough! She hasn't finished her training—"

"She's smarter than most beings," Anakin pointed out. "Loads smarter. She probably doesn't need more training."

Pala said, "Lord Tantos bought me. He wants to tutor me to be his private assassin."

"Oh, no!" Amee said. Wald swallowed. A loud gulping noise escaped from his green throat.

Anakin felt all the air go out of his lungs. This was bad news, the worst he had heard in a long time. Lord Tantos had a reputation for being ruthless.

Anakin, Kitster, and Pala had been friends for a long time. Gardulla the Hutt had owned all three of them once. Even though they'd been split up, they'd always lived in Mos Espa. They'd always been able to see each other. Now Pala would leave Tatooine.

"What can we do?" Kitster asked.

"Us?" Dorn said sarcastically. "Nothing, of course. If she tries to run, or tries to fight, all Madame Vansitt has to do is push a button, and *bang*!" The whiskers on Dorn's face and the hair around his ears all raised at once, doing a good imitation of a head exploding.

Pala shook her head. Dorn was right. Slaves all had bomb transmitters hidden beneath their skin. If they disobeyed their masters or tried to escape, it would mean the end of their lives.

Pala wasn't the type to run from her problems, but Anakin was concerned about this. He knew that they'd have to come up with some sort of a plan. "You're afraid of Lord Tantos, aren't you?"

Pala nodded.

Anakin wanted to do something, to save Pala if he could. "Can you show me Lord Tantos?" Anakin asked. If he could watch him for a little while, he might think of something.

Pala nodded. "He's in Derlag's Cantina."

Somehow Anakin had suspected that Pala would

know exactly where to find her new master. She really would make a good spy someday.

"Maybe I'll go have a look," Anakin said.

He turned to go, and Wald and Amee followed him. The crowd around the racers had thinned out a bit. But then Anakin remembered something. "Oh, no," he said. "I almost forgot to have a look in the crate!"

Kitster nodded toward the large blue doors that led to the loading docks. "The droids took the crate in there."

The big doors were closed, but one little side door was still open. Still, getting through could be a bit of a problem.

Gamorrean guards swaggered around, looking mean. The loading crew was still trying to lift the Podracer from its berth.

"Uh, you can't go in there," Wald warned Anakin.

"Sure he can," Pala offered. "I'll get him in there, if he's got the nerve."

* * *

Five minutes later, Pala let out a bloodcurdling scream. "Aaaagh! Help! Help!"

Anakin glanced across the far side of the landing bay. Pala leaped up and down. Her head-tails lashed like snakes as she screamed and clambered atop a pile of crates. Amee, Wald, and Dorn all started to scream, too.

Burly guards raised their weapons and took off running toward the children.

Taking advantage of the diversion, Anakin and Kitster raced through the small open door and dashed around a corner onto the loading docks.

They stood for a moment, afraid that they might hear the sound of the guards in their heavy armor behind them.

Pala shouted hysterically, "I saw a womp rat! I saw a huge womp rat!" Amee and Dorn joined in. "It ran behind those crates!"

The guards began laughing. There were plenty of womp rats around Mos Espa. But the Gamorrean guards weren't scared, even though the rats ate meat and would often attack people. Gamorreans thought that womp rats tasted great!

Anakin chanced a peek around the door. Sure enough, the guards were searching behind the crates for the womp rat.

He and Kitster crept into the darkened docking bay. The room was big enough to hold thousands of crates from a deep-space freighter. But Sebulba had only left one huge black crate in the room.

Anakin stared hard at it. There was something wrong with the crate. He could *feel* it, the way that he could feel a broken rotor in an engine, or corroded wires in a droid.

He hurried to get close, and heard a mechanical whirring noise and a crackle from the crate. The crate had air holes in it, near the top.

A sick feeling assailed him. He'd seen crates like this before. He'd heard the cries of slaves within, had smelled the sour odor of dirty bodies. He'd even been in one himself for awhile.

He peeked into the hole. Inside, the crate shimmered and pulsed with electricity.

"There's an energy cage in there!" Kitster said.

Anakin grunted. Energy cages were seldom used for transporting slaves. They were saved for dangerous criminals, or for creatures too monstrous and powerful to be shipped in a normal cage.

At first Anakin couldn't see much inside the cage. He squinted through an air hole. By the faint light, he made out tiny shapes inside the black crate. There weren't criminals inside, or monsters—there were only children, strange children with pale glowing skin, and bright eyes. They were beautiful, but frail and small, all lying on the floor of their cage. The children were covered with bruises.

Anakin suddenly recalled that energy cages were also used when transporting the most *valuable* of slaves.

"What *are* you?" Anakin whispered through an air hole.

A small girl, as thin as a shimmer tree, looked up at him with pale eyes. She brushed back a lock of silver hair. She looked young, maybe eight years old. "We're Ghostlings, from Datar. We've been kidnapped. Can you help us?"

"Kidnapped?" Kitster asked. "You mean you've been *captured*?"

"Kidnapped—taken from our parents," the girl said. "We want to go home. My name is Arawynne. Princess Arawynne."

Anakin shook his head. "Tatooine is your home now. You're slaves." It was best if new slaves learned to accept their lot in life.

"But...that's not right!" the girl said.

Kitster said, "Right or wrong, if you've got the transmitter implants, you have to do what your master says. If you don't, *boom*!" He made a noise like an explosion.

"Implants?" the girl asked. "We don't have any implants. We just got here. Please, help us. Open the crate!"

Anakin looked at Kitster. Even if he could get the Ghostlings out of the crate, he doubted that they'd be able to run far. But then again, maybe they wouldn't *need* to run far. If they didn't have implants yet, all they needed to do was to get on an outbound ship. Their masters wouldn't be able to track them.

Anakin didn't have time to form a plan. A gruff voice behind him shouted, "Hey! What are you doing here?"

He turned to see a Dug in the doorway.

Anakin and Kitster jumped down from the loading dock and raced toward the spaceport exit. Blaster bolts ricocheted off the floor near their feet. They were running for their lives!

CHAPTER FOUR

Khiss the Dug watched the figures flee. He fanned the docking bay with his blaster, checking for more intruders.

In seconds some Gamorrean guards reached his back, bearing clubs and crude blades. Khiss shouted at their commander, "You were supposed to be guarding this cargo bay!"

The Gamorrean grunted, making it clear that he'd take care of it. His men fanned out into the cargo bay as they headed for the far exits. It was all rather comical to Khiss. Obviously, the intruders were long gone.

Khiss strode over to the packing crate and looked in on the new slaves. The Ghostling children were alive. He quickly counted them off.

"Good to see you all here," Khiss said in his deep voice. The Ghostling children looked up at him. In unison they gasped in fear. His ugly face had a way of doing that to some folks.

"Please, can you help us?" one of the children begged.

Khiss smiled cruelly. "Help? I think not. You're worth a lot of money to my master. Ghostlings are hard to find."

"I didn't do anything bad!" one little boy cried. "I want to go home."

"We didn't take you because you're bad," Khiss said. "We took you because you are what you are."

Khiss worked for Sebulba. Khiss took orders for rare slaves of specific breeds.

You want a Bothan slave? That will be ten thousand, and no questions asked. You want a Columi? A hundred thousand.

Ghostlings...thirty thousand each.

After Khiss took the orders, Sebulba would use his tour of the galactic racing circuit as an excuse to stop at a world where the right kinds of slaves could be acquired.

There, Gondry and Djas Puhr would capture the slaves, hiding them on Sebulba's freighter.

Customs officials rarely inspected his ship. Those who did were almost always most interested in getting his autograph, or taking a close look at his Podracer. They never bothered to check the crates full of "spare parts" in his hold.

So it was easy for him to run his little slave-trading operation.

Trading slaves was a nice way for Sebulba to make pocket money. Not that he needed it. Sebulba was rich. He won more races than anyone else in the galaxy—and made more in prize money in a single year than most people made in a lifetime.

Still, Sebulba liked to keep his hand in all kinds of dirty enterprises. It kept his mind sharp.

At that moment, the giant Gondry ducked under the doorway and entered the docking bay, with Djas Puhr at his back. Djas Puhr was wearing a stylish visor over his face to cut out the harsh light of Tatooine.

"I smell blaster fire," Djas Puhr said. "What's going on? Why the security alert?"

"Intruders," Khiss said. "I found them messing with our slaves. I took a shot at them."

"What kind of intruders?" Djas Puhr asked.

"Small creatures, wearing hooded robes," Khiss reported. "They might have been Jawas."

Djas Puhr strode over to the cage, sniffed around it for a moment. "Not Jawas. Humans. I smell human children."

Djas Puhr looked into the cage through its air hole. "So, my Ghostling pets, what did the humans want? What were they after?"

None of the Ghostlings would answer. They all looked away. Djas Puhr could tell by her thoughtful expression that Ghostling Princess Arawynne was trying to come up with a good lie.

"Watch the cage well," Djas Puhr warned Khiss. "I smell more than human children. I smell trouble!"

CHAPTER FIVE

Anakin raced through the streets of Tatooine with Kitster at his side. He watched over his back, afraid that the Dug would come after them, firing its blaster.

They'd hardly gotten out of the spaceport when Watto came flying up the street. The Toydarian had an angry look on his face. "There you are! Where have you been? Slacking off with your friends? I've got a job for you."

"Uh, I was just trying to get a look at Sebulba's ship," Anakin said. "I had to sneak onto the docking bay to see his crate. One of his guards shot at me!"

"Really?" Watto asked. He rubbed the stubble on his chin. "Find anything interesting?"

Anakin shook his head. "It was just some slaves that Sebulba captured." He didn't tell Watto that they were helpless children kidnapped from their homes, or that they were frail creatures covered in bruises. Watto wasn't interested in that kind of thing.

"Bah," Watto said in a disgusted tone. "Look, I need you to go out to the Jundland Wastes and pick up a few things for me." He handed Anakin a keypad with a long list on it. "You'll do the bartering, then have the Jawas deliver the merchandise." Watto smiled cleverly. The Jundland Wastes were full of Jawas who were in the middle of their annual rendezvous. They were buying and selling items scavenged from the desert. Anakin was much better at getting good deals with the Jawas than Watto was.

Anakin looked helplessly at Kitster. Anakin wanted to free the Ghostling children, but he didn't even have time to talk with his friend about it—or make a plan. Instead he had to go off on another chore.

"It's okay," Kitster promised. "We can talk later."

Anakin took his sand skimmer to the Jundland Wastes. A sand skimmer was merely a board with a tiny repulsorlift engine on it. By pushing with one foot, Anakin could make the skimmer glide over the hardpan of the desert. By leaning left or right, he could steer.

It was slower than a speeder, but far faster than walking. In a couple of hours he reached a towering rock called "The Market." There, he found hundreds of sandcrawlers parked in the great rock's shadow.

The Jawas had spread their materials all over the ground—rusted, wrecked spaceships and skimmers, droids that had been caught in sandstorms, pieces of dew harvesters. It was an endless array of junk, but Anakin managed to find the things he needed within an hour. He even bartered the Jawas down to a good price.

As he did, he tried not to think too much about Pala being sold to the pirate lord, or of the Ghostling children caught in their energy cage.

He'd been longing for his own freedom for years, and the freedom of his mother. But like most slaves, freedom wasn't actually a goal that he could work for.

As the afternoon wore on, Anakin's tongue began to swell in his throat. The ride on his sand skimmer had been hot and tiring. He wished that he'd stopped at Jira's stand for a cool drink before he left Mos Espa.

He decided to wait in the shade until nightfall before trying to make the trip back to town. He desperately needed a drink, but he didn't dare buy one out here. Watto had given him a little money for some food, and the Jawas had plenty of things available—but all at outrageous prices.

Though he was hungry and thirsty, he settled for a hubba gourd. That way, he would have enough spare change to buy a little present for Pala before she left the planet.

The exterior of the hubba gourd was tough as stone, and covered with shiny crystals that reflected the sunlight. He broke the gourd open with a sharp rock to get at the pale, spongy fruit. It tasted bitter, but it put a little food in his belly and satisfied his thirst.

After he finished eating, he wandered through the maze of broken droids and harvesters, looking for a present for Pala—something special. Anakin found an old black jinapur root that was smoothed and polished by the desert sands, and bought it. He immediately began carving a good-luck charm from it as he wandered through the mazes of junk, and he kept his eye out for a little something more—maybe a metal chain to hang it from, or a cheap stone to set into it.

Twice he came back to one particular Jawa who had a huge Radon-Ulzer engine that was dented and rusted.

Anakin looked it over and felt sure he could make the engine run. He'd been building his own Podracer for years from scraps he'd gathered, but he didn't have any engines.

The Radon-Ulzer would have worked, but the Jawa insisted on selling it for cash. Anakin didn't have that kind of money.

As the suns began to set, Anakin felt bleak and defeated. He picked up his sand skimmer and began to make his way through the crowds of Jawas, through islands of junk and debris.

Then, that something special he'd been looking for finally caught his eye.

He stopped at a pile where an old Jawa silently leaned on a crooked stick. Its gloves were wrapped around the staff.

At its feet was an odd assortment of items— shiny blue stones from the edge of the Dune Sea, polished bones of Krayt dragons, a rope woven from bark. Among some pieces from old blasters Anakin noticed a very strange cube that looked to be far, far older than any piece of equipment that Anakin had ever seen.

He picked it up. The cube was small enough to fit in the palm of his hand, like playing dice. Intricate designs showed on its face, but the designs were so worn that they could hardly be recognized.

On one side of the cube, it looked like a picture of two Jedi Knights, fighting with lightsabers.

Another side of the cube showed a volcano. A third side was so worn that he couldn't tell if it had ever had a picture. A fourth side revealed a star map, with instructions on how to land on a certain moon. A fifth side was also worn smooth. A last side showed a lamp with a knife blade through it, the symbol of forbidden knowledge. Every corner of the cube had writing on it in some language that he couldn't decipher.

Anakin imagined that tens of thousands of people must have touched this cube over hundreds or thousands of years.

He hefted it, thinking that the cube was some sort of storage container. But it was so light that it had to be empty.

Yet, when he squinted, he could feel...well, there was something inside. Something...evil.

The cube had no latches on the outside, no locks or hinges that he could see. Anakin could almost imagine that the cube wasn't a box at all, but some component to a machine whose purpose had been forgotten ages and ages past.

"For you, very cheap," the old Jawa said to Anakin.

"What?" Anakin asked haltingly. The Jawan language was very hard to understand.

"Very cheap."

"But I don't want it," Anakin said. "I was just looking." He glanced toward home. It was getting late.

"Three credits," the Jawa offered, twisting the knob of his cane. It was exactly the amount that Anakin had in his pocket.

"No," Anakin said. "I don't even know what it is."

"Three credits is a small price to pay for knowledge," the old Jawa said. Under his gray-black hood, the Jawa's eyes gleamed.

"No," Anakin said. He started to put the cube down, but couldn't. What if it really was evil? What if it was dangerous—like a bomb or something? By just leaving it, he could be setting a trap for some unsuspecting person. It really *was* better to take the thing. Maybe Watto would know what it was.

In the deepening shadows, he took out his last three credits and handed them over to the Jawa.

On his way home, Anakin had nothing but starlight for company. He tried to open the cube a dozen different ways. He pushed on pressure points and threw it against rocks.

He began to imagine that it must have an electronic lock. Perhaps if he bombarded it with a magnetic wave generator, he'd hit the right frequency and get it to open.

But he knew that if something really important was inside, the box might be encoded. He might never get it open.

Anakin was asleep on his feet by the time he got home. As he reached the barracks, he felt happy to see that the light in the main room was still on. His mother was up waiting.

He opened the door and called, "Hi, Mom."

Anakin's mother, Shmi Skywalker, was up late, working to repair a maintenance droid. She had parts everywhere strewn upon a bench. "Oh, there you are," she said. Her voice was tired and full of worry. "At last."

"What are you doing?" Anakin asked. He couldn't imagine that Watto would have his mother up so late.

"You know my friend Matta?" Shmi asked. "She came down sick, and couldn't finish her quota of repairs today. I...was afraid that Master Dengula might sell her if she falls behind, so I brought this home to work on."

"If Dengula sold her," Anakin said hopefully, "it might not be so bad. He's a cruel master. She could hardly do worse."

"Yes," Shmi said, "but Dengula would never sell her to someone kind. It would only cause unrest among his other slaves. No, he's just the kind who would sell her to the spice mines of Kessel."

The spice mines of Kessel were a slave's nightmare. The glitterstim spice mined there was far underground, and any exposure to light ruined it. So the miners had to work in total darkness, digging, digging, digging with their hands. And there were monsters in the mines that crept up on people and ate them.

Shmi balled her fists up angrily and glanced at her son. Anakin knew that he must have looked tired. She said, "Well, don't you worry about it. Get some sleep."

Anakin could hardly think about sleep. He thought about the Ghostling children, locked in their cage for the night, waiting to be fitted with detonators. He thought about Pala scheduled to leave the day after tomorrow.

He was worried about them, just as his mother was worried about Matta. The only difference was, he couldn't do anything to help Pala or the Ghostlings. Could he? If there was any way at all—he would have to try.

"I'm not that tired," he said. "I'll stay up until the droid is fixed."

He went to the worktable and glanced at the parts, mentally sifting through them, deciding what to do first. His mother couldn't fix things as well as he could.

Shmi Skywalker rubbed his shoulder and said in gratitude, "Thank you. Whenever we do something kind, it makes all of the problems in the universe shrink a little."

Anakin looked up at his mother. The universe was so full of problems, and all of them seemed so much bigger than Anakin.

Yet when he blinked, when he closed his eyes, he imagined that he was in the hold of a spaceship, that Pala and the Ghostling children were all around him, and he could hear the sound of engines rumbling and feel the familiar sensation of flight.

It was just like being in a Podracer, hurtling through the canyons, where dangerous walls of rock reared on every side.

Except that in this dream, he knew that something grand waited beyond the finish line. There was freedom for Pala and the Ghostling children.

It was so real, for a moment he almost thought he saw it, tasted it, felt it. He was flying free with Pala and the Ghostling children.

He blinked away the waking dream, and got back to work fitting the droid pieces together.

"Mom," he asked. "What if you want to do something good, but it's hard? Or what if you want to help someone, but you're afraid?"

Shmi smiled down at him. She closed the droid's service panel. "Helping others isn't always easy, is it? If people paid us to be good, the galaxy would be overflowing with kindness. But most of the time there isn't much reward, and sometimes it even costs us dearly to do good things."

"Yeah," Anakin said. "What if it costs so much that it hurts?"

"I think we should do it anyway," Shmi said. "Make it a habit, like eating or breathing. Once you do, you'll hardly even notice the cost."

When they finished the droid, Shmi got out some cold dinner for Anakin. He ate and drank a little, then went to bed. His mom kissed his forehead and whispered, "Go to sleep. The suns come up early, and we'll have a long night tomorrow. Matta's still sick."

CHAPTER SIX

In her cage, Princess Arawynne cuddled with the little ones. At seven years of age, Arawynne didn't know much about how to be a princess.

She knew that princesses were responsible. She knew that they led their people. But where could she possibly lead the young ones?

Borofir, the youngest boy, was only three years old. He had black, curly hair, and his eyes were deep blue. All through their trip, he'd sucked his fingers and cried for his mama. Arawynne didn't know what to tell him, other than to promise that he'd get to see her again soon. She begged him to stop crying, and mostly, he did.

All of the children here were younger than Arawynne. Conno was five; Alamar, the oldest next to Arawynne, was only five and a half.

The pull of gravity had been light on their old planet Datar. There, Arawynne had weighed much less than she did here on Tatooine. She found that she got tired if she tried to stand up in her cage for very long. Sometimes it was hard to breathe.

No wonder humans from other worlds seemed strong! Ghostlings were very frail in comparison.

Her captors had not given the Ghostling children much food or water. She'd had to divide it as best she could, and Arawynne didn't take much for herself. Her stomach growled loudly.

"Mama? Daddy?" Borofir cried. He stirred in his sleep, then got up to his knees, looking around. If he'd been back home, he would have had his mother and father sleeping with him in his nest. He'd merely have to feel for them.

Arawynne wished that she had a blaze bug to give a little light, so that she could see better.

"I'm here," Arawynne whispered. She squeezed Borofir's small hand. "It will be all right."

"I want to go home," Borofir begged.

"We'll go home soon," Arawynne replied.

But she had no way of keeping such a promise. She was locked in an energy cage and had no idea how to get out. Worse than that, she had been moved to Gardulla the Hutt's fortress. Gondry was still guarding them, and beyond the doorway she could hear other guards stirring from time to time, as well as the sound of heavy-sounding doors sliding open and closed.

Desperately she thought about the boys who had looked through the air holes to her cage earlier today. She'd hoped that they'd free her. A small part of her still dared to hope.

She wished that she were a Jedi, with knowledge of the Force. She thought of the boys and tried to imagine sending her message across the gulf of space. "Please," she silently begged, "come set us free."

But she knew that they would not come. Because the boys were only slaves themselves.

CHAPTER SEVEN

Kitster had a secret.

In fact, Kitster had lots of secrets, and he was good at keeping them.

There was one secret that he'd never told anyone —not even his best friend, Anakin. And if he ever told anyone, he'd probably be killed for it.

Kitster knew who his own father was.

When Kitster was a child, he recalled being aboard his father's warship. His father was a pirate of sorts, named Rakir Banai. Some called him a pirate, some said that he was something more, something of a lawman who worked not for any government, but to satisfy his own sense of justice. He traveled along the trade routes here on the untamed rim of the galaxy, where slavers and spice lords abounded. He'd capture their ships, free their slaves, steal their money, and destroy their payloads.

For that, Rakir Banai was a hunted man. All of the Hutt crime lords had placed bounties on his head.

When Kitster was four, he'd been aboard a pirate ship that some bounty hunters captured. Kitster and his mother were separated and sold as slaves. She'd warned him, "Never tell anyone who you are. Never tell them who your father is. And never forget who you are—or how much I love you."

So at age four, Kitster was caught and sold. He had no idea who his mother was sold to, but Kitster was sold to Gardulla the Hutt. That's where he first met Anakin and Pala.

It was a good thing Kitster was great at keeping secrets, because he'd learned a good one today.

After Anakin had to run off to work, Kitster, Pala, and Dorn watched the loading bay at the spaceport to find out where the Ghostling children would be taken.

Pala and Dorn were both good watchers. Madame Vansitt had trained Pala to be a spy, and Dorn's owner, Jabba the Hutt, was doing the same for him. Dorn was a Bothan, after all. They made the best spies in the galaxy.

Pala and Dorn had seen something interesting: Gardulla the Hutt had purchased the Ghostling children. They'd all been taken to Gardulla's fortress, just outside of town.

Kitster lay awake in his bed, his head whirling, as he considered that piece of news. He couldn't imagine why Gardulla, his own master, would want such creatures. The Ghostling children were very expensive, and they didn't have any skills at all. They weren't good fighters. They wouldn't make good guards or warriors. They weren't any smarter than other species. So why had Gardulla gone to so much trouble to capture them?

All that they had was a rare and special beauty unlike anything that Kitster had ever seen.

He was lying on his cot in the slave quarters thinking about it when he heard a faint noise, a tapping on his wall: *Tap, tap,* pause. *Tap. Tap. Tap.*

That was Dorn's signal. The Bothan boy was out-side Kitster's room. How had he gotten into Gardulla's fortress?

That was dangerous. If Dorn got caught sneaking around here at night, he'd be in *big* trouble! Like any criminal, Gardulla also had secrets to hide and treasure to guard.

The other slaves were all snoring in their sleep. A dozen slaves were kept in nearby rooms. Kitster was afraid that one of them might wake.

He crept to the front door and pushed the OPEN button.

As soon as the door hissed open, Dorn ran through in a crouch, holding a small bundle in his hands. He hit the CLOSE button, and the door snapped shut.

Both of them stopped for a moment, to see if they'd attracted any attention.

Dorn went to a nearby table, dropped his bundle next to a small computer terminal. It was a mess of wires all attached to a small keyboard. It looked like the kind of thing that criminals used to break elec-tronic locks.

"What's going on?" Kitster whispered.

"I've been thinking about those new slaves, the Ghostlings," Dorn whispered in reply. The little Bothan spy raised his long eyebrows at a tilt then dropped them quickly. Kitster didn't know Bothan body language, but suspected that he was saying, *as I'm sure that you have.* "I thought maybe we could find out what Gardulla wants them for."

"What are you going to do?" Kitster asked.

Dorn put a finger to his mouth, warning Kitster to be silent, then snapped a clip onto the cable of the computer terminal. The terminal had the "house" systems on it. It regulated the temperature, monitored for fires and intruders, and occasionally used its electronic eyes to scan the quarters so that it could send cleaning droids when needed—or simply to look for slaves.

Now, Dorn rapidly began typing on his keyboard, and the computer screen faded. In seconds the light reappeared, but instead of the normal household menu on screen, there was a list of options that Kitster had never seen.

"You've hacked into Gardulla's main terminal!" Kitster whispered in amazement.

"It's all part of one big system," Dorn said casually. He began typing really fast now, and information flew across the screen. Bothans have quick eyes, and Dorn seemed to read ten times faster than Kitster.

In moments Dorn turned to Kitster and said quietly, "Interesting. Did you know that Gardulla is building a huge underground pleasure garden? It will have open ponds, streams, and imported trees."

"Yeah, everyone knows about it," Kitster said. It was going to be perhaps the most extravagant garden on Tatooine, a place with rich, moist air where the wealthiest scumbags on the planet could gather for parties. It was the kind of place that Hutts liked. "So what does that have to do with the Ghostling children?"

"Gardulla wants to put them in her garden."

"As caretakers?" He could hardly imagine that the Ghostlings would make good workers. They were far too frail. Just touching a Ghostling bruised it.

"No, more like lawn ornaments," Dorn said in an angry tone.

Kitster let out an astonished gasp. It wasn't such an odd idea. Slave owners often paid more for beautiful slaves—pretty young girls to serve their drinks, handsome men to guard their rooms. But kidnapping children in order to use them as lawn ornaments seemed...excessive, even on this corrupt planet.

"The thing is," Dorn lowered his voice and whispered in a dangerous tone, "Gardulla is going to put other creatures in the garden—animals that could hunt the Ghostlings. Those kids won't last a year."

Kitster was hardly shocked by the idea. Hurting helpless creatures made the Hutts feel strong. Gardulla had killed expensive slaves before, often to show guests how powerful she was. It was a savage entertainment.

"Gardulla's doctor is scheduled to come in the morning, to implant the transmitters. If we're going to save the Ghostlings, we'll have to do it tonight."

Kitster's mouth was dry, and his palms were sweaty. He hadn't really thought about trying to save the Ghostlings. He'd never tried to free a slave before. He knew what would happen if he got caught.

"Where—"

"They're in the dungeon, in the hospital," Dorn whispered. "You want to try it?"

Kitster knew Gardulla's dungeons well. He'd spent time down there before. You couldn't just walk in and walk out. There were droid guards and Gamorreans, electronic gates and keyed gates.

"We'd never make it," Kitster said. "We're just kids!"

"Pala could help," Dorn said with a wry grin. "And Anakin." Pala was good with computers and spy equipment, and she was an excellent liar—almost as good as Kitster. And Anakin was a wizard with anything electronic. Yeah, they were all kids, but they were *special* kids.

Kitster thought fleetingly of Wald and Amee. They might be willing to help, too. But almost immediately he had to reject the idea. They might have the guts for this kind of thing, but not the training.

"What do you say?" Dorn asked. "Are you in?"

"We could get caught. We might get killed."

"I dare you," Dorn said with a grin.

And Kitster...Kitster's specialty was sneaking around. He was always sneaking away from work, sneaking back into work.

"I double dare you," Dorn said.

"All right," Kitster whispered. "Let's give it a try."

At this point, you must decide whether to continue reading this adventure, or to play your own adventure in the *Star Wars Adventures* Game Book, *The Ghostling Children*.

To play your own adventure, turn to the first page of the Game Book and follow the directions you find there.

To continue reading this adventure, turn the page!

CHAPTER EIGHT

Anakin and his friends, Dorn, Kitster, and Pala, glided on their sand skimmers along the dark streets of Mos Espa toward the Palace of Gardulla the Hutt.

An eopie's squawk echoed from the pour-stone walls of the slave quarters. Elsewhere, Anakin could hear a heavy clanking.

Though it was late, the cool wind on his face helped wake him. Dorn had roused him from a dead sleep and had outlined his plan to save the Ghostling children.

"All right, I'll help," Anakin had agreed, though he knew it was dangerous.

Really, he was just returning something that had been stolen. But could he really ever return the children? They were from Datar. They had no way to pay for their passage home. How would he ever get them back to their parents?

Dorn and Kitster had brought him a Jawa's robe made of sandstone-red homespun fibers. Anakin could smell the vermin odor of the Jawa who'd worn it.

Dorn had done more than dress them like Jawas. He'd brought light patches to put above their eyes so that if anyone looked under the hood, they would think that they saw a Jawa's glowing eyes. Anakin even wore gloves, so that his hands looked like a Jawa's.

It was just like Dorn to have these disguises.

Kitster had a description of the dungeon, and knew what guards were on duty. He told his friends where to meet if there was trouble. He'd even brought a Jawa's ion blaster to disable any droid guards. Pala was pulling a repulsorlift sled, so that they could bring the Ghostling children back to town once they got them out.

Soon, they neared Gardulla's Fortress.

Jagged peaks rose up from the desert like teeth in a rotted, overturned skull. The fortress squatted atop them like a giant spydr. The huge black central dome of the fortress could open to receive space-ships. To Anakin, it looked like a spydr's back. Then, down among the jagged peaks, were black towers of synth-steel that had gun emplacements on them. Anakin imagined that these were legs to the spydr.

But the building was only part of the fortress. Legend said that it was built atop an old mine. Tunnels and caves riddled the hills beneath the monstrous fortress. He remembered vaguely that it was a maze down there.

As he stared up at the insectlike building, he filled with despair. *How would they ever get the Ghostling children out?*

CHAPTER NINE

Silently, Anakin and his friends streaked over the hardpan toward Gardulla's fortress, hugging the shadows beside a pile of rocks. They stayed hidden from anyone on the palace walls. Red lights on the fortress dome reminded Kitster of bloodshot eyes—searching, searching.

It was good that the lights looked like eyes. It reminded Kitster of the fact that there were very real sentries on the walls. There were guard droids inside whose only purpose was to stare over the walls and emit a shrill whistle if anything odd approached, or if anyone tried to escape.

Like any child who knew the place well, Kitster had several ways to sneak in and out. In fact, Kitster probably knew more ways to be sneaky than anyone else. But doing so without being seen could be a problem.

A few shadows were all that hid them.

Kitster took the lead, letting his sand skimmer hum over the dry sand. Ahead, a narrow chasm split the rocks, where desert winds had eroded a passage. An adult on a speeder couldn't have made it through, but it was just right for a kid.

"Keep your heads down," Kitster whispered to his friends. "Watch out for the rocks! There's razor moss growing on them."

He expertly glided through the narrows of the chasm. Long white funnel flowers protruded from crevices above, making soft breathing noises as they inhaled the night air, trying to get moisture.

Kitster kicked the ground to build up speed. Rock walls on either side seemed to fly past. Here and there, hubba gourds grew on the ground. Their faceted husks reflected the starlight.

He rounded a turn. Something big and dark huddled on the trail. At first he thought a boulder had fallen, but the thing lifted an ugly head. It emitted a fierce growl.

"Cliffborer worm!" he shouted to the others.

Cliffborer worms only came out on Tatooine at night. This one was probably feeding on the razor moss, or sucking water from the hubba gourds. With one good bite, a cliffborer worm could suck a gourd—or a person—dry.

Kitster leaned left. The sand skimmer tilted away from the cliffborer worm's sharp teeth—right against the stone wall of the canyon.

The cliffborer worm wriggled toward him. Kitster kicked hard and sped up.

Rrraarggh! The huge worm lunged. Kitster whipped by so close that he could smell its hot breath. He slapped its head.

The cliffborer worm snarled in rage and lunged at him—too late. It banged its head into the rock.

Kitster kicked the ground again, gaining speed, and glanced back. The cliffborer worm shook its head, trying to regain its senses, as Anakin slid through the narrows.

Kitster didn't watch what happened. He had to watch the path ahead. Where there was one cliffborer worm, there might be more.

He hurtled through the narrows until at last they opened wide, into a small valley.

"Keep to your left," he whispered to the others. "Stay in the shadows. We're right under the fortress walls."

He hardly needed to tell them. Up above the fortress loomed, a black monolith in the night. Red lights from windows high overhead gleamed evilly. He could hear faraway music, Kloo horns that wailed like human screams, drifting from the room.

Now they slowed their sand skimmers, creeping, until the cliff met the wall of Gardulla's palace.

They dismounted.

They were directly below an opening. About twenty meters above, there was a vent that let the hot air escape from the castle. Kitster had come down earlier through the vent. There were iron bars over it, meant to keep people out, but he'd long ago sawed through one of the bars, making a hole big enough to climb through. He'd left a grappling hook wedged between two iron bars.

He hoped that no one had found the grappling hook, or had learned of his escape. He reached out and felt along the wall. The fibercord from the grappling hook met his hand.

"Here," he whispered. He found the reel on the ground and hooked it to his belt.

Just then, he heard an electronic whir up above, atop the wall. He flattened against the wall just as a guard droid wheeled to a stop. He heard its hydraulics as it turned its mechanical head, peering over the ledge.

He held his breath, terrified that the droid would see them.

After a long time, its engines whirred, and the droid continued its rounds.

Kitster pushed a button on his reel. The reel lifted him quickly up the wall.

He neared the top and climbed into the vent. The air coming through it was only a little warm. The fortress had been cooling for hours.

He hit the release on his reel and played the fiber-cord out until his friends could grab it. Soon, they all wiggled between the bars and climbed into the vent.

Kitster led them as they crawled through the round passage of the vent. They crawled on and on, past the kitchens and the laundry rooms, and beyond the sleeping quarters of Gardulla's henchmen. He slid down a side vent off of the pool room.

Here were several large swimming pools, some with waterfalls and fountains. Sometimes Gardulla actually swam in one of the pools. Other times she would stock a pool with carnivorous fish and have guards toss in anyone who had displeased her.

Kitster sat quietly for a moment before he entered the room. He doubted that anyone would be there at this time of night, but he didn't want to take a chance. A grate fit over the vent. He couldn't see past it. Glowrods near the ceiling gave off only faint light.

Every sound echoed through the room. Waterfalls tumbled softly. Kitster heard the skittering feet of a big insect, and he figured that if the shy bug was foraging for dinner, the room had to be empty.

The air smelled heavily of water. He waited for the others to reach him. He whispered, "If we get split up, meet me back here."

He hoped they'd be able to find their way back if they did get split up. It had been a long time since Anakin or Pala had been in the fortress. The corridors down here in level seven were a maze. When this hill had been mined, the miners struck off in any direction they wanted. There were side passages that led nowhere, empty rooms, switchbacks, and dead ends.

Gardulla kept the new slaves penned in down here simply because it was such a confusing place. It was mighty hard to escape.

Kitster opened the grate quietly and dropped to the ground. He stepped away to make room for the next person, then crouched. Anakin leaped down behind him, then Pala and Dorn.

Overhead, the glowrods near the high ceiling looked like slivers of stars. Potted plants beside the pools formed a screen between the kids and the water. In some places, huge boulders had been placed for decoration.

Kitster slunk beside a pool, quietly making for the main door.

"Hmmmm?" a deep voice bellowed from the water nearby. Something huge stirred in the pool, making a splash.

There, floating on her back, was Gardulla the Hutt!

"Who's there?" she asked absently in Huttese.

The Hutt was wallowing in the shallows like a small whale. Her enormous head was propped up on a rock, her eyes closed to slits. She'd been half-asleep.

Behind Kitster, Anakin and the others came to a halt. Someone's feet slapped the pavement loudly.

"Uh, it's me, O Great Mistress," Kitster said, speaking the Hutts' native language and disguising his voice. He didn't give a name. Gardulla had so many servants that she didn't know the names of them all.

"Ahhhhhh," she groaned pleasantly. "Get the scrub brush for my back. It itches."

"Yes, O Wisest of the Wise," Kitster said. He peered around in the dark for a scrub brush, and saw a huge one at the edge of the pool. It had a handle as tall as a Wookiee, and its bristles were as hard as steel.

He got the heavy thing and wondered what to do. Kitster didn't want to be seen. He was disguised as a Jawa, and Gardulla never let Jawas into the fortress. She was afraid that they might steal something.

But even as Kitster stood there in a panic, Gardulla began to snore. Kitster set the brush down and tried to sneak away.

Gardulla's own snoring wakened her. "What? What?" she blustered. "Where's that brush?"

"Coming," Kitster said. Gardulla's eyes immediately began to close. Kitster dragged the brush over to Gardulla. Kitster lifted it and began scratching Gardulla's back.

The Hutt groaned pleasantly and closed her eyes. Kitster looked over his shoulder at his friends, still hiding behind the plants. He jutted his chin toward the door, and they began to creep away.

"Aaaah, that feels good," Gardulla crooned.

Kitster tried to do the job, but in moments his arms began to tire. It was hard work. The pavement beneath his feet was wet and slippery. A huge container of liquid cleanser sat by his feet, and some of it had spilled onto the pavement. Kitster was afraid he'd fall in.

He had to get out of there!

CHAPTER TEN

Anakin's heart was racing as he crept from the pool room into the main access tunnel. Dorn and Pala followed.

Anakin stopped in the hall. He didn't know his way to the slave pens. Kitster's directions hadn't helped much. The main corridor here was simply a rough rock wall, painted white. There were passages everywhere, often with big security doors bolted crudely over the openings.

Still, it felt familiar. Anakin remembered something of this place from his childhood.

Gardulla was a trader. She didn't raise slaves, and she didn't train them. She kept hundreds of slaves on her staff, but she bought and sold thousands more as fast as she could.

Most of her slaves went to mining companies on harsh worlds. The companies bought them in bulk. "We need two thousand workers for the moon on Gedi Four," an order might say. Gardulla would fill the order any way she could.

So the dungeons might be filled with thousands of slaves one day, and be empty the next.

Tonight they were lucky. Kitster said that a new shipment of Whiphids had just come in from Toola. The mangy creatures were still half-wild. They were as mean as...well, there wasn't much that was meaner.

Most of the guards would be down in the maximum-security pens.

Anakin had hoped that he and his friends might be able to just walk to the infirmary and free the Ghostlings. But apparently that wouldn't happen.

"What now?" Pala whispered.

"You wait here," Dorn answered. The Bothan pointed left down the hallway. "I'll scout ahead." Dorn handed Anakin the Jawa ion blaster and tiptoed toward a far door. He reached it and thumbed the entry switch. It was locked.

He pulled out some wires and his keyboard, clipped the wires to the switch, and punched in some numbers. The door slid open.

He shot a grin back to Anakin and Pala. Anakin shifted his grip on the ion blaster. His palms were sweating.

CHAPTER ELEVEN

Dorn was lost.

He'd sneaked down the hallways, thinking he'd reach the slave pens, and he'd managed to open a number of locks.

Suddenly he opened a door and found row after row of cages. They weren't filled with the slaves he was searching for.

They were filled with giant bugs.

Enormous bugs. *Lots* of them. There were poisonous ghost spydrs from Kubindi, bigger than some houses he'd seen. There were giant two-headed effrikim worms—a Hutt's favorite snack—three meters long. There were mora beetles with giant horns on their noses, pounding their cages.

Obviously, these weren't normal bugs. Gardulla had a gourmet chef from Kubindi, one who specialized in cooking insects. But of course such a chef couldn't have just any insects. These ones were bred for size and tastiness, and had probably been fed chemicals to make them mutate into gigantic forms. Afterward, they'd probably been injected with growth hormones.

The stink of alien bugs made Dorn's nose twitch. The insects began to hiss and chitter. The beetles blew a noise from their horns that sounded like "Flee. Flee."

They wanted him to leave. Dorn didn't have a better idea.

CHAPTER TWELVE

Finally, the Hutt's breathing eased, and she looked asleep. Kitster pulled away the huge scrub brush. He set it down, and turned to creep away.

"Hmmm, that felt good," Gardulla boomed. "But now I'm hungry. I want a little something to eat. How about you?"

She wants me to have dinner with her? Kitster thought. That didn't make sense. A Hutt would never invite a slave to dinner. On the other hand, Gardulla was known to eat a slave from time to time.

Yikes! Kitster thought.

Before the danger fully registered in Kitster's mind, there was a little splash, and one of Gardulla's strong arms snaked up. The Hutt grabbed his ankle.

"Augh!" Kitster shouted as Gardulla pulled him toward the pool. She was going to eat him!

Kitster landed hard on the pavement. Gardulla yanked him toward her mouth.

Kitster looked for something to hold onto. The only things handy were the huge scrub brush and the liquid cleanser.

He grabbed the cleanser and glanced backward. Gardulla's huge mouth opened to meet him.

Kitster sprayed the soap down Gardulla's throat.

The mighty Hutt roared in outrage. "Agghhh! Help! It's poisoned me!"

Gardulla let go of Kitster's ankle and began to clutch her throat. The Hutt began spitting out soap, her enormous tongue rolling comically.

Kitster sprang to his feet.

He raced for his life as Gardulla roared in fury, "Guards, help! I've got cleanser in my mouth!" Her enormous voice echoed from the ceiling and seemed to fill the whole fortress.

From the hallway outside the pool room, Kitster suddenly heard his friends shriek in alarm!

* * *

Meanwhile, in one of the corridors, Anakin glanced at Pala.

Her head tails, hidden beneath her Jawan cloak, twitched nervously. The movement made it look as if she had some small animals climbing on her back.

They'd been waiting for a long time. Dorn had been gone for a while, and Anakin was beginning to think he wasn't coming back.

But the only thing to come down the main corridor was a mouse droid. It stopped nearby and began to use its tiny arms to scrupulously pick up specks of debris.

"Wow," Pala whispered, nodding at the mouse droid, "Gardulla sure keeps a clean dungeon. She's a credit to her slimy species."

Anakin grinned.

Suddenly he heard a splash from the pool room. He heard Kitster scream. Gardulla began to shout.

A door flung open at Anakin's right. A Gamorrean

guard thudded into the hall, stun baton drawn. The mouse droid squealed and blurred past Anakin's feet.

Anakin drew his ion blaster. Gamorrean males are short on brains. This one saw the blaster and cringed in terror, not knowing that ion blasters are only good on electronics. It wouldn't hurt the Gamorrean. So Anakin didn't pull the trigger.

He turned and fled after Pala.

They raced past the door that Dorn had opened, then rounded a corner. The Gamorrean chased them. His armor jangled. He sounded like a tank driving down the hall.

The guard was running too fast. Anakin couldn't stay ahead of him. So he hid around the corner.

The guard raced after him, and Anakin stuck his foot out.

The Gamorrean tripped and landed with a thud, as if a load of garbage had fallen off a lifter.

Anakin ran after Pala. The guard got up and began to chase them again.

Behind them, Kitster sprinted out of the pool room, heart pounding. He heard a Gamorrean guard rushing down the hall to his left, chasing Anakin and Pala.

But the noise was distant, far away. It echoed through the stone corridors, and Kitster couldn't tell which way to go.

Kitster ran for a bit, down passageways that he knew well. But when he found the long corridor to the slave quarters empty, he realized that Anakin and Pala had made a wrong turn.

His friends were lost.

Somewhere in the fortress, he heard a giant mora beetle blowing its nose horn, "Flee! Flee!"

He thought quickly.

Many of the doors to the maze were locked. Given the direction that he'd run, and the doors that Kitster had seen open, Anakin must have turned left down the slave's corridor when he needed to go right.

"Oh no!" Kitster whispered to himself. "They're heading toward the security control room!"

CHAPTER THIRTEEN

Dorn was about to leave the bug room when he heard a shout. Gardulla was calling for her guards.

Dorn thought, *You know, the great thing about giant mutant bugs is that they're a lot smarter than most people give them credit for. I mean, I'll bet they know that Gardulla plans to eat them, and they probably resent it.*

"Hey, you guys," Dorn offered the bugs, "If I let you out, would you promise to wreck this place good?"

None of the bugs answered. He'd hoped for some kind of nonverbal answer—a flip of the antenna, a nod of the head. Dorn was great at reading nonverbal cues.

The problem with the bugs was that he wasn't sure if they'd heard his offer at all. *Where are the ears on a ghost spydr, anyway?* he wondered.

Dorn heard a Gamorrean out in the main corridor.

He found the control panel for the cages and pushed the buttons to open the doors.

A huge beetle leaped out of its cage and charged into the main corridor, its nose horn blaring, "Flee! Flee!" It slammed against the wall of the corridor, and looked as if it might just sit and batter it for awhile. Then it caught sight of the Gamorrean rushing toward it.

The beetle wheeled to its left, lowered its nose horn, and charged the Gamorrean. The Gamorrean guard screamed. He turned and ran, grunting with every breath.

Dorn leaped into the hall just in time to watch the giant beetle ram the guard from behind. The Gamorrean slid on his belly and hit the wall headfirst, driving his iron helmet over his eyes. The giant beetle charged round a corner, looking for another victim.

Dorn whispered under his breath, "And I thought Jabba's palace had bug problems!"

The Gamorrean guard crawled to his knees, and tried to pry the cap off his head.

Dorn turned and fled.

* * *

Anakin was panting. He knew he'd taken a wrong turn somewhere, but this way *felt* right.

He reached a T in the hallway, then turned to see several droids marching toward him, fresh from an oil bath.

"Ah!" a protocol droid cried on seeing him. "Jawas with ion blasters!" The droid raised its hands over its head and began hopping around in terror.

Anakin just stood, not knowing what to do. If he neutralized them, it would be cruel. If he didn't neutralize them, the droids might call some guards.

"Please, don't shut me down," the protocol droid begged. "My gyro balance circuitry will be thrown off for days! Here, have my locomotor—I'll give you anything you want."

The droid began opening his forward access panel.

"Utini!" Pala shouted to Anakin in Jawa. "Let's go!" She pulled Anakin around and raced down the left half of the T. The droids all began shouting, "Help! Help! Jawas!"

This isn't going the way I thought it would, Anakin realized with dread.

He came to a door marked SECURITY, and punched a button.

The door slid up, and he had a brief glimpse inside. A horribly scarred man in a dark gray uniform was sitting at a desk. He was studying some monitor screens on the wall. One of them showed Dorn in a room, releasing hundreds of giant bugs from their cages.

"Jawas," the man was muttering in concern. "Thieving little rats." He reached for a red button marked ALARM.

Anakin pulled up his ion blaster and fired.

Blue circles of ionized gas hurtled from the blaster and hit the control panel. Sparks erupted from the panel. Monitors on the wall exploded. The guard ducked to avoid the flying glass and caught sight of Anakin.

"You dirty little Jawa!" he screamed in rage. He pulled a heavy blaster from his holster.

Pala did the only thing that a reasonable person could do in such a situation. She hit the CLOSE button on the door. It whisked shut just as the guard pulled his trigger.

Anakin heard the *ping* of the blaster bolt ricocheting through the room. Then there was a dull *thud* as the security guard plopped to the floor.

"Oh no," Anakin exclaimed in terror. "I hope he's not dead!"

"Maybe we'd better hope that he *is* dead," Pala corrected. She grabbed his arm. "Come on, I think we need to go this way!"

Anakin, Pala, Dorn, and Kitster reached the door to the slaves' infirmary at the same time.

Farther back in the fortress, Anakin could hear Gamorreans yelling. Someone had discovered the giant bugs. That would keep them busy!

Dorn pulled out his electronic lock overrider and quickly got the infirmary door open.

The infirmary was dark. Bacta tanks, lighted from beneath and filled with water, bubbled in one corner. Beds filled the middle of the room.

In a corner was the energy cage, with the Ghostling children inside. The cage looked like a simple black platform, but a shimmering blue haze surrounded it. The Ghostling children all lay on the platform, sound asleep.

In front of the cage stood a guard—a great big cyclops from the planet Byss.

The giant scrutinized them with its huge eye, and growled in its best approximation of Huttese, "Hey, what are you Jawas doing here?"

Anakin's heart froze. He didn't know much about giants from Byss, but he'd heard they were practically impossible to kill, and they were as dumb as rocks.

Anakin strode to the front of the door to distract the giant while Dorn unhooked his overrider from the circuitry.

Anakin answered in a high voice, as if he were a Jawa who had somehow mastered Huttese, "You go. We guard prisoners."

The cyclops opened its eye wide in delight. "Really?" Anakin could tell that no one had ever bothered to relieve it from guard duty before. People always treated dumb giants from Byss as if they were...well, dumb giants from Byss.

"Go now. We guard," Anakin repeated.

The huge cyclops lumbered out the door, much to everyone's relief.

Anakin rushed over to the cage. The locking mechanism on it looked very sophisticated. As he knelt to study it, one of the Ghostling children stirred in her sleep—the girl he'd spoken to earlier that day.

She glanced up at Anakin and instantly came awake. She carefully disentangled herself from the children she'd been holding. She tried to get up, but she was badly bruised, and she gasped in pain. As she climbed to her feet, the children began to stir. "Wake up," she told them. "We're getting out of here!"

Anakin watched the frail Ghostling children with rising concern. They'd had a rough trip here, and all of them were badly bruised and injured. He'd imagined that they'd all run off with him, but now he wasn't so sure.

Anakin heard the sound of booted feet running down a side corridor, out in the hallway. Some Niktos were shouting in their crude language, listening to a communicator.

Kitster closed the door. They all knelt quietly as the Nikto guards ran past.

Anakin could hear part of the Niktos' conversation over the communicator as they sprinted past. "There's a mora beetle chasing Mistress Gardulla around in the pool," someone warned. "But watch the south corridor. Ghost spydrs are stringing webs everywhere!"

Anakin was trembling. He'd hoped to sneak into the compound quietly and save the Ghostling children without anyone knowing. Now the whole fortress was as busy as a Ferrelian ant hive.

"Oh no," Dorn said as he knelt by the door. "We just locked ourselves in! And I can't get at the electronic wires from in here!"

"Here, get me out of this cage," Arawynne said. "I know how to get us out of this room!"

Dorn ran over with his overrider kit, clipped it to the cage's electronic lock, and got to work. It was a long process. The lock on the energy cage was a tough one to open. Sweat glistened on his forehead.

"How can we get out of here?" Anakin asked Arawynne.

"Blow the door open!" Arawynne said. Blowing the door open sounded dangerous. Someone might get hurt. Besides, it was sure to attract unwanted attention.

"Blow it open with what?" Pala asked.

"Look over on the counter. There's a box of transmitters," Arawynne said. She pointed to a small box on the counter. They were the same transmitters that Gardulla's doctor was going to implant in Arawynne and the others. "We can use those to blow up the door."

Anakin ran to the box. The transmitters were small wafers about the size of his thumbnail. The black exterior was made of axidite, and a set of numbers was painted on it.

A white component of the transmitter housed some circuitry. Anakin was good with electronics.

The white piece had to have a small receiver in it. That way, when Gardulla sent a signal to the transmitter telling it to blow up, it would blow up.

There were dozens of transmitters in the box. With them, lay a transmitter that carried the numeric codes.

Boy, Anakin thought. *I sure wish I could put one of these transmitters in Gardulla! If I did, she'd treat everyone better from now on!*

He picked up a transmitter, memorized the number, and carried it to the door. He wedged the wafer between the door and wall, up by the electronic lock.

Just then, Dorn got the energy cage to turn off. The shimmering blue field of energy disappeared.

Arawynne and the Ghostling children were free. Now, he had to get them to safety.

"Everybody watch out!" Anakin said. He got the little transmitter and pushed in the code numbers. He made sure that everyone was well-hidden behind walls and operating tables, and then pushed the SEND button.

The transmitter roared. Flame filled the passageway, and the door evaporated into dust. Smoke filled the room.

Anakin raised his head above the operating table. He stared wide-eyed at the gaping hole.

Now he knew what he'd look like if the transmitter in his own body ever exploded.

"Hurry!" Kitster shouted. "We have to get away from here before the guards come."

"Where to?" Dorn asked.

"The Ghostlings won't be able to run far or fast," Anakin warned.

"I've got to think." Kitster held his head in terror. "No matter which way we run, the security cameras will spot us!"

"No they won't," Anakin promised. "I shot them with my ion blaster."

"Great! I have an idea," Kitster said. "Let's go!" He began to lead the Ghostling children from the room as fast as he could.

Anakin grabbed the box of transmitters and the receiver, shoving them into his pocket. They might come in handy later.

Kitster quickly led the children to a nearby elevator. As the door closed, he heard the sound of booted feet rushing down the hall toward the infirmary.

A smoke alarm began blaring. *Breeep. Breeep. Breeep.*

He closed the elevator door, and just stood for a moment, thinking.

With all of the guards coming down to sublevel seven, the best thing to do was to take the elevator up, away from the danger.

But that would just leave them stranded higher on the mountain.

Even a short run had left the Ghostlings winded, out of breath. They were from a world where the gravity was far lighter than here. They'd never be able to run all the way to the exit. They'd never be able to make the trip to town, either.

Kitster doubted that he and his friends could carry them all. Besides, even touching one of the Ghostlings left them bruised.

He looked up, catching Pala's eyes. "Where to?" she asked.

He couldn't think of a plan, not an easy one.

"Maybe we can fly out of here," he said. He pressed the elevator button, launching it up six floors.

"You're crazy," Pala objected. "We can't fly!"

"We've got to find some way to get the Ghostlings to safety," Kitster objected. "Anakin could fly. He'd be a good pilot."

The elevator stopped, and the door opened into the air hangar. They were under the huge dome of the fortress. There were dozens of ships here: Corellian freighters, light cruisers, even a couple of Z-95 headhunters. Maintenance droids worked single-mindedly fueling and cleaning the ships.

The domed roof, which could open to let ships in and out, was closed for the night.

Anakin looked at the dome, and at the ships sitting quietly. "It won't work," he said. "We'd have to get the dome open in order to fly out. And as soon as we did, Gardulla's gunners on the towers would shoot us down. We'll have to sneak out. We'll have to find another way."

Kitster looked back at Arawynne. One of the Ghostlings, a small boy, was sobbing.

"How far do you think you can run?" Kitster asked. It was a long way from here to the vent, where they'd stored their weapons.

"Not much farther," Arawynne said.

Pala offered the only sensible answer to the problem. "We'll have to hide them for now and come back later. But where?"

Kitster thought quickly. There were dozens of places —one of the ships nearby, or one of the storage rooms. But those areas would be searched first, and most thoroughly. Besides, there was no telling how soon he could come back to get them.

Kitster answered, "I've got an idea. Come with me!"

He led them across the flight deck, and through a hallway beyond. He figured with bugs downstairs, Jawas, and explosions, everyone in the fortress would be looking for them down below. There was one place that they wouldn't suspect.

He led them all to a huge iron door that was almost never used, and pressed a button.

The door whisked open, and with it came the smell of fresh air, trees, water, moss, and rocks. The dome above was covered in transparisteel that let in the starlight. In that light, Kitster could see the twisting trunks of trees. Huge luminous moths danced in the air above some flowering vines. Fans stirred the air, and in the distance he could hear running water.

"Welcome to Gardulla's pleasure garden," Kitster announced.

"But didn't you say that there are animals in here that eat people...or Ghostlings," Pala objected.

"Not yet," Kitster said. "Not for months. Gardulla's foresters aren't done. They've been working all season, planting trees and flowers, and now they're almost done. They're Ho'Din."

The Ho'Din were a peaceful people from the planet Moltok. Their very name, Ho'Din, meant "walking flowers." They were tall and lean, with gorgeous red and violet scales that hung from their heads like hair. They loved nature.

Kitster would be willing to bet his own life that the Ho'Din would help hide the Ghostlings. Indeed, he *was* betting the lives of the Ghostling children.

Something pale, like an ugly spydr, crawled toward them through the door.

"No animals you say?" Dorn asked. "I wouldn't go in there with that."

"That's not an animal," Arawynne corrected. The Ghostling Princess knelt and picked the thing up. "It's called a knobby white spydr, but it's not really a spydr. It's more like a seed—a seed that walks. It pulls itself off of a gnarltree. Then it goes looking for a place to plant itself."

"We can't have them stay in there," Pala said. "It's spooky."

"If there are gnarltrees," Arawynne said, "then it will feel like home. There will be good places to hide, down among the roots."

"I'll come back for you," Kitster promised Arawynne and the children. "I'll bring you food. And when the excitement has died down, I'll figure out how to get you home."

"We all will," Anakin promised.

Arawynne stared at her rescuers for a long moment, and choked back a sob. "Thank you," she whispered very graciously. "Thank you." She gathered the children and led them into Gardulla's pleasure garden.

CHAPTER FOURTEEN

Kitster led his friends through the fortress. They climbed through more air vents and ducts, through abandoned tunnels that few people knew about.

Only Kitster's knowledge of the fortress saved them.

At one point, Anakin had to use transmitter caps to blow up a guard droid, just to create enough of a diversion so that he and his friends could get out of a jam.

It seemed that everyone in Gardulla's fortress was awake, searching for the Ghostling children. Anakin and his friends were constantly running, hiding from the sounds of approaching guards. Kitster snuck back to his quarters, wishing his friends luck.

Anakin was afraid that someone would come up behind him, so every once in awhile he'd hide the tiny transmitters on his trail—wedging them between cracks in the rock, tossing them onto the floor where mouse droids might pick them up, or dropping them down air shafts.

An hour before dawn they were creeping through an old mine shaft toward Gardulla's pool room when Anakin heard the sound that he dreaded most.

In a long tunnel behind him, he heard the repulsor engines of a seeker droid—a floating ball, made specifically to hunt down runaway slaves.

Seeker droids have lots of expensive sensors in them—sniffers, DNA sequencers. If this droid had his scent, there was no way that he'd escape! It could hunt for him all across Tatooine, even if it took years.

Worse than that, behind the seeker droid, he heard the march of iron feet. Bigger droids were following the seeker, and they'd have ion shielding. There was no way that he could fight battle droids with his Jawa ion blaster.

In desperation, Anakin tossed the rest of the box of transmitters to the ground and shouted, "Run for it!"

There was only one way to escape. He had to set the detonators off all at once, blowing the seeker droid into such tiny pieces that it could never be repaired.

His friends sped toward the pool room. Anakin reached it, too. But while his friends all raced for the vent, he stood beside the door, detonator in hand, and punched in the command to blow up all of the transmitters at once.

He glanced back into the corridor.

The seeker droid glided around the corner, coming toward him. Its chemo-receptors were extended, and its electronic eye swiveled like a searchlight. It spotted him and let out an electronic squeal, warning the battle droids behind.

Six battle droids leaped forward into the corridor, heavy blaster rifles in hand. As one, they knelt and opened fire.

Anakin darted for cover behind the doorway. Blaster fire swept through the pool room in a glowing barrage. He checked to make sure that his friends were all right.

Pala and Dorn were safely across the room, out of the line of fire, climbing into the air vent. But they weren't out of danger yet. Anakin had to destroy those droids!

He gritted his teeth and waited until the blaster fire stopped. The seeker droid hummed and began to glide toward him. The battle droids marched behind it.

He listened hard, trying to tell where they were in the hallway behind. He had to time his attack just right.

There was a part of himself that Anakin was just beginning to learn to touch, a sense that he had not yet mastered. Sometimes, when he was racing his Podracer, he could let himself go, simply feel the path ahead.

Now he fought to calm himself, to touch that peaceful center. He listened hard for the sound of the droids, but sounds were tricky down here in the tunnels. The curve of the tunnel and the uneven ceilings made it hard to judge distance by sound alone.

He waited until he thought it was almost too late. Then he pushed the SEND button.

Fire filled the tunnel, and the whole mountain fortress seemed to groan. Scraps of the seeker droid and battle droids shot past Anakin so fast he couldn't even judge what they'd been. Smoke roiled from the cave, and the ground trembled violently. In some places, he could tell, entire caverns were collapsing. Gardulla's palace continued to tremble.

Anakin raced to the air vent. Smoke burned his eyes, and the vent became unbearable. He crawled through as quickly as he could, holding his breath.

When he reached the opening, he didn't have time to sit and wait or to worry about whether he might be seen. He had to get out of the vent, get to fresh air.

He grabbed onto the fibercord and dropped over the edge of the wall, letting himself down as quickly as he dared, hand-over-hand.

Only then did he look up to see if he'd been spotted.

A Jawa sandcrawler was rolling over the desert past the fortress, its huge treads creaking. It looked like it was heading toward the rendezvous out by Market Rock. It made a rumbling noise like distant thunder.

From the upper walls of Gardulla's fortress, a gunner fired a blaster cannon. Perhaps he thought that the Jawas were coming to attack in full force, given the disturbance that Anakin and his friends had caused.

Blue bolts streaked through the night sky and ricocheted harmlessly from the heavy armor on the sandcrawler. The sandcrawler lumbered away.

The noise and confusion provided a distraction for Anakin and his friends to make their escape.

They landed at the base of the fortress, and looked up. Smoke was rising from Gardulla's palace in a dozen places. Anakin doubted that anyone would be looking for him out there.

They headed into the desert, and soon split up. Anakin, Pala, and Dorn rode to town on their sand skimmers.

All the way home, Anakin thought about what he had risked to save the Ghostling children.

If anyone ever found out what Anakin and his friends had done—*boom*. That would be the end of them all.

He hadn't accomplished everything he wanted, but he'd done some good. The Ghostling children weren't free yet, but at least they were hidden. They didn't have the detonators planted in them. And maybe, if they were all lucky, the Ghostling children would all be able to go home.

He tried to imagine the tears of joy that would be shed if they made it home. Think of it, to be home in the arms of your own mother and father after such a terrible ordeal.

And most amazing of all, to be free!

That was something that Anakin couldn't imagine. It was something that he wished for everyone—for the Ghostling children, and for Pala, who would be sold off the planet tomorrow.

The children separated once they reached Mos Espa. Anakin and Dorn each gave Pala a hug. They said good-bye.

Anakin promised to come see Pala before she flew off with Lord Tantos.

By the time Anakin reached his own bed, it was almost time to get up.

His eyes felt gritty, and he laid down on the bed for a long time, so tired that he couldn't move.

Soon, he thought. *Soon I'll get up.*

At this point, readers who chose to follow the adventure in the *Star Wars Adventures* Game Book can return to the novel, *The Ghostling Children*.

CHAPTER FIFTEEN

Sebulba the Dug stood before Gardulla just after sunrise the next morning. They were in the Hutt's reception hall, with dozens of guards around. Gardulla appeared to be angry. She was lying upon a vast purple throne, smoking a huge pipe full of glitterstim spice.

"So, O Great One," Sebulba said in Huttese. "I have delivered the Ghostling children, and now I must bring up the indelicate matter of...payment."

"Ho, ho, ha!" Gardulla the Hutt laughed, a deep booming sound. "Now I see your trick. I should have known!"

"Trick, O Incredible One?" Sebulba asked in his most servile manner. "What trick?"

"The slaves are gone," Gardulla said. "They escaped during the night. At first I wondered who might have stolen them. But who would be so foolish as to steal slaves from the Mighty Gardulla? I'm onto your trick."

"Stolen? Trick? The slaves are gone?" Sebulba snarled in disbelief. "Impossible! I had Gondry watch them!"

"Hah!" Gardulla bellowed. "You practically admit it. You had your own man 'guard' the children. I'm sure it made it so much *easier* to steal them. But I see through your plan. You hoped to get me to pay for them *now*, then pay again *later*. What treachery! I'm going to kill you!"

"Kill me?" Sebulba said, hoping it was a bluff. "If you did, who would you bet on at the next Podrace? Admit it, my old friend: I'm worth more to you alive than dead."

Gardulla's eyes opened wide as she considered Sebulba's point. "What treachery," the Hutt mused. "What...*admirable* treachery." The Hutt roared in laughter. "But your plan didn't work."

Gardulla wriggled down from her throne till she stood before the scrawny Dug. She pointed a beefy finger at Sebulba and raised herself to her full height. "Nice try, Podracer. But if you want payment, you'll have to deliver the children."

Sebulba was furious. His mind was racing.

Where could the children be? Gondry had said that Gardulla sent her own men to relieve him of duty —an unlikely story. But...could it be that someone had aided the Ghostling children in their escape?

Sebulba gazed evenly at the Hutt.

Finding the children would be hard for most people. But Sebulba had Djas Puhr to hunt for him. With Djas Puhr's keen nose and night vision, few slaves had ever eluded him for long.

"I will get the children back," Sebulba vowed. "And *soon*!"

NEXT ADVENTURE:
THE HUNT FOR ANAKIN SKYWALKER